I0830770

KITCHEN

OF TIME

The Kingdom of Time Cookbook

Luz Evan Kanin

Cover design by Amy Frerichs
Cover copyright © 2025 by Luz Evan Kanin
Interior design by Luz Evan Kanin
Illustrations by Amy Frerichs
Author photograph by Bella Photography

First Edition: November 2025

Printed in the United States of America

ISBN: 979-8-9933199-2-6

For all the hunger-addled girlies and their mouths

full of fangs.

Scroll of Savor

Lastisap Latte

(Time: 10 mins, Servings: 2)

Dry Ingredients

3 chai tea bags
¼ tsp ground all spice
½ tsp ground cinnamon
½ tsp ground ginger
¼ tsp ground cloves
¼ tsp ground nutmeg

Wet Ingredients

2 cups water, boiling
1 ½ cups milk
¼ tsp pure vanilla extract
4 tsp pure maple syrup

Directives

1. In a large measuring cup, combine the dry ingredients, vanilla extract, and maple syrup. Pour the boiling water over the spice mixture and steep for 5 minutes.
2. While the spice mixture steeps, heat the milk in the microwave for 75 seconds. The milk needs to steam but not boil.
3. Place the frother into the hot milk and turn it on. Slowly raise the frother to just below the milk's surface until it starts to swirl. Continue frothing until the desired amount of foam has formed.
4. Pour 1 cup of the steeped tea mixture into a large mug. Then, holding the milk foam back with a spoon, pour ¼ cup of the liquid milk into the tea mixture. Repeat with second mug.
5. Lastly, top each mug with the desired amount of foam, dust with cinnamon, and enjoy.

Midnight Goldspice

(Time: 5 mins, Servings: 2)

Wet Ingredients

1 ½ cup water, boiling
3 oz cinnamon whiskey
1 lemon, 2 tbsp lemon juice
2 tbsp raw honey
½ tsp pure vanilla extract

Garnish (Optional)

2 lemon slices, seedless
2 cinnamon sticks

Directives

1. Slice the lemon in two and squeeze the juice from one half into a mug over a strainer. Repeat with the second mug.
2. Add 1 ½ oz cinnamon whiskey, 1 tbsp honey, and ¼ tsp vanilla extract to each mug.
3. Pour ¾ cups boiling water into each mug, stir until honey is fully dissolved, add optional garnish, and enjoy.

POLICE

Cocktail a la Cesspool

(Time: 5 mins, Servings: 2)

Wet Ingredients

4 oz Midori liqueur
4 oz soda water
2 limes, 2 tbsp lime juice
1 lemon, 2 tbsp lemon juice
2 ice spheres

Garnish (Optional)

2 lime slices, seedless
2 cocktail cherries

Directives

1. Pour 2 oz Midori liqueur into a lowball glass. Repeat with second glass.
2. Add 1 tbsp lime juice and 1 tbsp lemon juice to each glass and stir.
3. Add one ice sphere into each glass, top with 2 oz soda water, add optional garnish, and enjoy.

Bristol's Banana Bread

(Time: 75 mins, Servings: 8)

Dry Ingredients

2 cups all-purpose flour
½ cup granulated sugar
½ cup brown sugar
1 tbsp ground cinnamon
1 tsp baking powder
1 tsp baking soda
1 tsp sea salt

Wet Ingredients

½ cup unsalted butter, softened
½ tbsp pure vanilla extract
2 large eggs, room temp
4 bananas, ripened
1 tbsp whole milk

Mix-Ins (Optional)

¾ cup milk chocolate chips
¾ cup chopped pecans

Directives

1. Preheat oven to 325°F.
2. Grease 8 ½ X 4 ½ bread pan.
3. In one bowl, combine dry ingredients (except white and brown sugar).
4. In another bowl, cream butter, white sugar, and brown sugar.
5. Beat eggs and vanilla into butter/sugar mixture.
6. Fold bananas and milk into butter/sugar/egg mixture.
7. Slowly fold dry ingredient mixture into butter/sugar/egg mixture.
8. Add optional mix-ins.
9. Pour combined mixture into greased bread pan.
10. Bake for 60-70 minutes or until toothpick comes out clean.
11. Cool and enjoy.

Everly's Blueberry Soulcake

(Time: 60 mins, Servings: 8)

Dry Ingredients

2 cups all-purpose flour
2 cups blueberries, fresh or frozen
½ cup granulated sugar
½ cup brown sugar
1 tsp baking powder
½ tsp sea salt

Wet Ingredients

2 tbsp unsalted butter, softened
½ cup whole milk
1 large egg, room temp
2 tsp pure vanilla extract
½ cup sour cream
1 lemon, 2 tbsp lemon juice

Glaze (Optional)

1 cup powdered sugar
2 tbsp water
1 tsp pure vanilla extract
1 tsp lemon juice

Directives

1. Preheat oven to 350°F.
2. Grease 8 ½ X 4 ½ bread pan.
3. In one bowl, cream sugars, butter, and remaining wet ingredients.
4. In another bowl, combine flour, baking powder, and salt. Stir until mixed.
5. Slowly add dry mixture into wet mixture. Avoid overmixing.
6. Fold blueberries into combined mixture.
7. Pour combined mixture into greased bread pan.
8. Bake for 65-75 minutes or until toothpick comes out clean.
9. While cake is cooling, whisk glaze ingredients together until smooth.
10. Once cake has cooled, drizzle glaze over the top and enjoy.

Muffins de Maelstrom

(Time: 30 mins, Servings: 18)

<u>Dry Ingredients</u>

2 cups all-purpose flour
1 ½ cups granulated sugar
½ cup unsweetened cocoa powder
1 ½ cup semi-sweet chocolate chips
1 tsp baking soda
1 tsp sea salt

<u>Wet Ingredients</u>

1 cup Greek yogurt, room temp
½ cup heavy cream, room temp
2 large eggs, room temp
1 tbsp espresso, room temp
1 ½ tbsp pure vanilla extract
½ cup vegetable oil

<u>Mix-Ins (Optional)</u>

¾ cup chopped pecans

<u>Directives</u>

1. Preheat oven to 425°.
2. Grease 12-count muffin pan.
3. In one bowl, combine dry ingredients and stir until mixed.
4. In another bowl, combine wet ingredients and stir until mixed.
5. Slowly fold wet mixture into dry mixture. Add optional mix-ins. Avoid overmixing.
6. Spoon combined mixture into greased muffin pan.
7. Bake for 5 minutes, reduce heat to 350°F, then bake for 20 more minutes or until toothpick comes out clean.
8. Let muffins cool before removing from pan, then enjoy.

Valiantly Vanilla

(Time: 45 mins, Servings: 4)

Dry Ingredients

4 cups all-purpose flour
2 tbsp granulated sugar
1 ½ tbsp baking powder
2 tsp baking soda

Wet Ingredients

4 cups buttermilk
4 large eggs
2 tbsp unsalted butter, softened +
more for cooking
½ tbsp pure vanilla extract
1 lemon, 1 tbsp lemon juice

Mix-Ins (Optional)

1 cup semi-sweet chocolate chips
1 cup blackberries

Directives

1. In one bowl, mix dry ingredients (except sugar) together.
2. In another bowl, cream eggs and sugar. Stir in remaining wet ingredients.
3. Slowly fold wet mixture into dry mixture. Avoid overmixing.
4. In a skillet or griddle, melt 1 tbsp of butter over medium-high heat.
5. Pour batter onto pan in 5-inch circles. Cook 2-3 minutes or until bubbles begin to form, add optional mix-ins, and flip pancakes. Cook another 2-3 minutes. When centers spring up to the touch, pancakes are ready.
6. Add butter to skillet and repeat.
7. Drizzle pancakes with syrup and enjoy.

Oh, So Sourdough Starter

2-lb bag whole wheat flour
7 cups filtered water

Day 1: combine 1 cup whole wheat flour and 1 cup filtered water,
stir vigorously, cover with tea towel, and leave for 24 hours.
Day 2-5: discard half the mixture and repeat Day 1 process.
Day 6-7: repeat Day 2 process every 12 hours instead of 24.
Day 7: starter is active when doubled in size and bubbling.

Oh, So Sourdough

(Active Time: 1 hour, Total Time: 36 hours, Servings: 6-12)

Dry Ingredients

3 ½ cups all-purpose flour
½ cup active starter, bubbling
2 tsp sea salt

Wet Ingredients

1 ¼ cup water, warm

Directives

1. Feed sourdough starter 8 hours prior to making dough.
2. In a large glass bowl, combine dry and wet ingredients. Stir until mixed, cover with plastic wrap, and leave for 30 minutes.
3. Uncover bowl and fold dough, pulling the edges up and out before folding them into the center. Rotating bowl, repeat three more folds. Repeat entire process two more times, waiting 30 minutes between rounds. After last round, cover bowl with a damp towel and leave in a warm place until dough has doubled in size. This can take 6-12 hours.
4. After dough has doubled, fold it into a ball on a floured surface. Leave dough ball uncovered for 20 minutes. Then flip it over and fold again, pinching the edges together in the center. Place dough, pinched seam up, in a floured bowl and cover with plastic wrap. Refrigerate for 15 hours.
5. Preheat oven to 500°F and heat dutch oven for 1 hour.
6. Just prior to baking, remove dough from fridge, place on parchment paper, score to suit, then add to preheated dutch oven. Refix dutch oven lid, place in oven, and bake for 20 minutes.
7. Lower oven temp to 475° F, remove dutch oven lid, and bake for 15 more minutes or until golden. Cool and enjoy.

Sempedormir Smear

(Time: 5 mins, Servings: 4)

Dry Ingredients

3 tbsp brown sugar
½ tsp ground cinnamon
¼ tsp ground all spice

Wet Ingredients

4 oz cream cheese, room temp
¼ cup heavy cream
½ tsp pure vanilla extract

Directives

1. In a small bowl, mix all ingredients until smooth.
2. Enjoy smear atop bread, toast, bagels, or as a fruit dip.

Almonds to Atone

(Time: 2.5 hours, Servings: 12)

<u>Dry Ingredients</u>

2 puff pastry sheets
2 cups granulated sugar
1 cup powdered sugar
1 cup almonds, blanched
1 tbsp ground cinnamon
1 tbsp lemon zest

<u>Wet Ingredients</u>

2 large eggs, 1 yolk
1 tbsp whole milk
1 lemon, 1 tsp lemon juice
1 tsp pure almond extract

<u>Directives</u>

1. Add 1 cup granulated sugar, almonds, cinnamon, and lemon zest into food processor and pulse until mixture appears sandy. Avoid over-pulsing.
2. Add egg yolk, lemon juice, and almond extract and pulse until cohesive.
3. Scoop mixture from food processer, cover in plastic wrap, and refrigerate for 2 hours.
4. On a lightly floured surface, roll out cold puff pastry sheets. Cut each sheet into six rectangles.
5. Remove filling from fridge and spoon onto center of each rectangle.
6. Fold one edge of the pastry over the almond filling, then fold the opposite edge back over the first and pinch. Repeat with each pastry.
7. In a small bowl, beat the remaining egg and milk, brush across tops of folded pastries, and sprinkle with granulated sugar.
8. Refrigerate pastries for 30 minutes.
9. Preheat oven to 375°F and grease cookie sheet.
10. Remove pastries from fridge, place on greased cookie sheet, and bake for 25 minutes or until golden.
11. Once cooled, dust pastries with powdered sugar and enjoy.

Perk-Up Pork Belly

(Time: 45 mins, Servings: 4)

Dry Ingredients

1 lb thick-sliced pork bacon
1 cup brown sugar
½ cup granulated sugar

Directives

1. Preheat oven to 425°F.
2. Line cookie sheet with parchment paper.
3. In a large bowl, combine sugars and stir until mixed.
4. Dip each slice of bacon into sugar bowl making sure to coat each side.
5. Place each coated slice onto the parchment paper lined pan.
6. Bake for 30 minutes, draining the fat and flipping halfway through.
7. Cool and enjoy.

Chicken Apple Saus-y

(Time: 45 mins, Servings: 12)

Dry Ingredients

1 lb boneless, skinless chicken breast,
chopped & frozen
½ lb boneless, skinless chicken thigh,
chopped & frozen
½ lb thick-sliced pork bacon,
chopped & frozen
3 Granny Smith apples, peeled,
chopped, & squeezed dry
2 tsp black pepper
2 tsp sea salt
½ tsp ground cloves
½ tsp ground nutmeg

Wet Ingredients

2 tbsp unsalted butter, cold
2 tbsp olive oil for cooking

Spices (Optional)

½ cup jalapeño, diced
½ tsp ground cayenne

Directives

1. Add apples into food processor, pulse 3 times, and transfer to large bowl.
2. Add half the chicken into food processor, pulse until coarsely ground, and scrape into apple bowl. Repeat with the second half.
3. Add bacon and butter into food processor, pulse until coarsely ground, and scrape into apple-chicken bowl.
4. Stir apples, chicken, and bacon together until well mixed.
5. Add spices and optional mix-ins to mixture and stir until well mixed.
6. Shape mixture into 12 equal balls then flatten into patties.
7. Heat olive oil in large skillet over medium-high heat.
8. Fry patties until golden, about 4 minutes on each side.
9. Cool cooked patties on paper towels and enjoy.

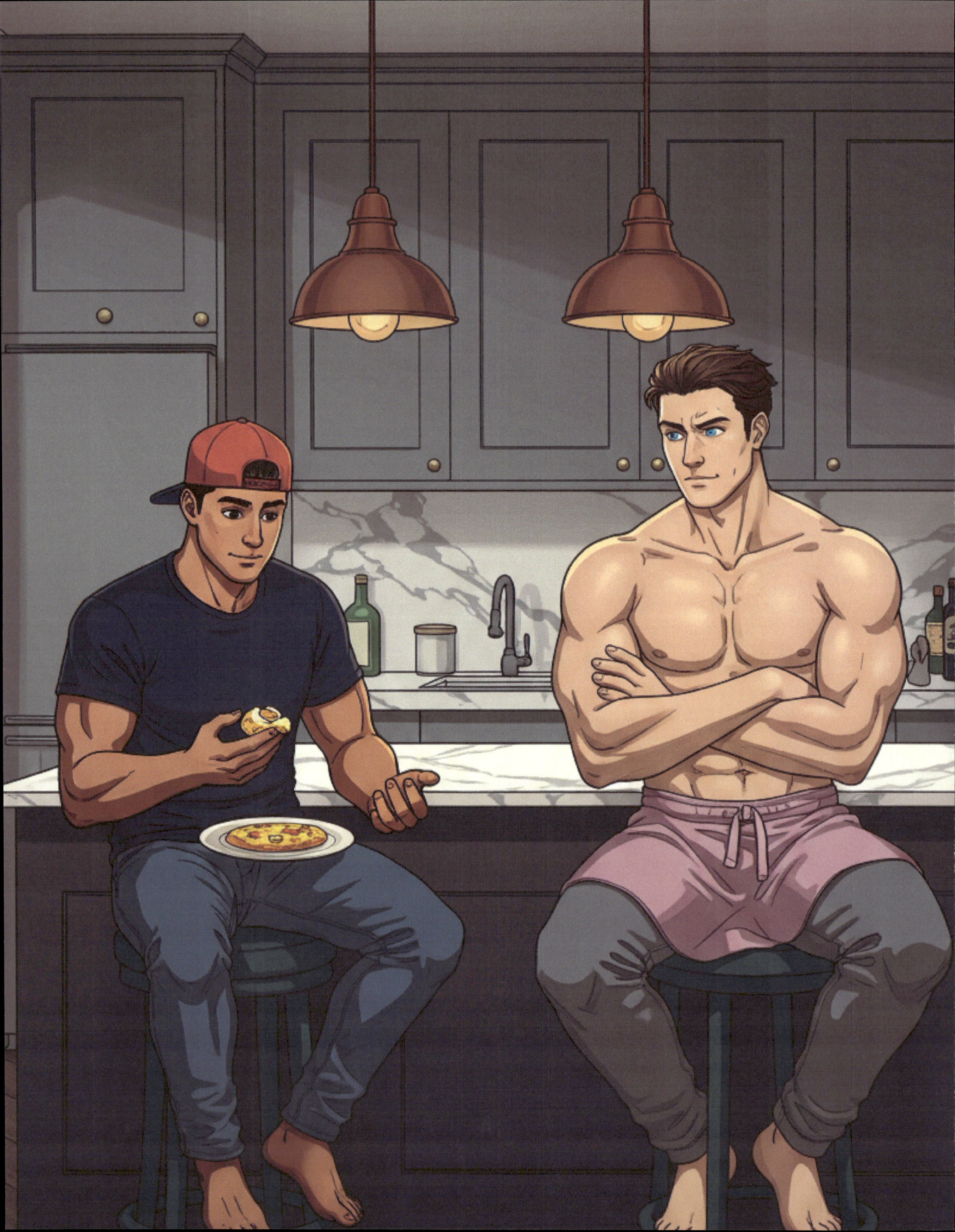

Let's-Be-Friends Frittata

(Time: 30 mins, Servings: 6)

Dry Ingredients

2 cups baby spinach*
1 ½ cup cremini mushrooms, sliced*
½ cup white onion, diced*
½ cup shredded parmesan
1 tsp sea salt
½ tsp black pepper

Wet Ingredients

2 tbsp olive oil for cooking
2 tbsp whole milk
2 tbsp heavy cream
10 large eggs

*can be substituted for kale, bell peppers, or zucchini

Mix-Ins (Optional)

1 cup pork or turkey bacon, cooked & chopped

Directives

1. In a large bowl, whisk milk, cream, eggs, parmesan, salt, and pepper.
2. In a cast-iron skillet, heat olive oil over medium.
3. Sauté onions until translucent. Add mushrooms and sauté for 2 minutes. Add spinach ½ cup at a time, draining between each add, and cook 5 minutes more.
4. Spread cooked veggies evenly across bottom of skillet then pour whisked egg mixture on top. Ensure egg mixture reaches bottom of skillet.
5. Gently stir in any optional mix-ins.
6. Place lid on skillet, reduce heat to medium-low, and cook for 10 minutes.
7. Set oven to broil.
8. Remove lid from skillet, place on center rack, and broil for 4 minutes or until frittata center is firm and golden.
9. Cool and enjoy.

Sad Strained Yogurt

(Time: 5 mins, Servings: 1)

<u>Dry Ingredients</u>

¼ cup fresh blackberries
¼ cup fresh blueberries
¼ cup fresh raspberries
1 tsp ground cinnamon

<u>Wet Ingredients</u>

1 cup Greek yogurt, vanilla
1 tbsp raw honey

<u>Directives</u>

1. Scoop yogurt into bowl.
2. Add honey and cinnamon and stir until well blended.
3. Top with fresh berries and enjoy.

On-The-Go Gyro

(Active Time: 30 mins, Total Time: 24.5 hours, Servings: 6)

Marinade

4 tbsp Greek yogurt
3 tbsp lemon juice
2 tbsp olive oil
1 tbsp white wine vinegar
1 tbsp raw garlic, minced
1 tbsp dried oregano
1 tsp sea salt
1 tsp black pepper

Tzatziki

1 ½ cup Greek yogurt
¾ cup cucumber, chopped & squeezed
2 tbsp olive oil
1 tbsp lemon juice
1 tsp raw garlic, minced
¼ tsp sea salt
¼ tsp black pepper

Filling

6 pita bread wraps
2 lbs boneless, skinless chicken thigh, chopped
3 tomatoes, chopped
2 cucumbers, peeled & chopped
½ red onion, peeled & diced
¼ cup fresh parsley, chopped
olive oil for cooking

Directives

1. Combine marinade ingredients in large plastic bag, seal, and massage until mixed. Unseal to add chicken, reseal, then massage until marinade has fully coated chicken.
2. Refrigerate marinating chicken for 24 hours.
3. In one bowl, combine tzatziki ingredients and stir until mixed.
4. In another bowl, combine filling ingredients (except pita and chicken) and stir until mixed.
5. Heat 2 tbsp olive oil in a large skillet over medium-high heat.
6. Remove chicken from plastic bag, add to hot skillet, and cook for 3-4 minutes on each side or until golden. Set chicken on plate to cool.
7. Microwave pita wraps for 30 seconds before placing on sheets of foil.
8. Spoon filling, chicken, and tzatziki into the warm pita wraps, roll like a burrito, secure with the foil, and enjoy.

Pizza Parlor Surprise

(Active Time: 2 hours, Total Time: 27 hours, Servings: 10)

Dough

4 ½ cups bread flour
1 tbsp granulated
sugar
1 tbsp sea salt
2 tsp instant yeast
2 cups water, warm
3 tbsp olive oil

Sauce

1 can whole peeled
tomatoes
1 white onion, peeled
& halved
1 tbsp olive oil
1 tbsp unsalted butter
2 tsp raw garlic,
minced
3 sprigs fresh basil
2 tsp dried oregano
1 tsp sea salt
1 tsp black pepper
1 tsp granulated sugar

Toppings

4 cups shredded
mozzarella, cold
6 oz pepperoni
2 tbsp hot honey
1 tsp sea salt

Optional

½ cup pineapple,
diced
½ cup black olives,
sliced

Directives a la Dough

1. Add bread flour, sugar, salt, and yeast into food processor and pulse to mix. Add water and olive oil and pulse for 30 seconds.
2. Scrape mixture onto a floured surface, knead until smooth, and divide into two equal portions.
3. Place each dough portion into a plastic bag and refrigerate for 24 hours.
4. Remove from fridge 3 hours prior to baking pizza.
5. Remove dough from plastic bags and fold into balls, pulling the edges up and out then pinching together at the top.
6. Roll each ball in flour, place in separate bowls, cover with plastic wrap, then set aside to rise until doubled in size.

Directives a la Sauce

1. Add tomatoes into food processor and pulse until puréed.
2. Heat olive oil and butter in a large skillet over medium-low heat. When butter has melted, add garlic, oregano, salt, and pepper and cook for 3 minutes, stirring constantly.
3. Raise heat to medium-high and add tomato purée, onion halves, basil sprigs, and sugar. When sauce begins to simmer, reduce heat to low and cook for 1 hour, stirring occasionally.
4. Remove sauce from heat, discard onion halves and basil, and cool.

Directives a la Pizza

1. Preheat oven to 500°F.
2. Roll out each dough ball into 10-inch circles. Carefully stretch circles until they are 16-inches wide and ¼-inch thick, then place onto pizza pans.
3. Spread 1 cup of sauce evenly atop dough, leaving a 1-inch border around the edge. Sprinkle 2 cups of mozzarella over the sauce. Top the cheese with pepperoni and any optional toppings. Repeat with second pizza.
4. Bake for 15-18 minutes or until crust is golden.
5. Remove pizzas from oven, drizzle with hot honey, sprinkle with sea salt, slice, and enjoy.

Wise Guy Wieners

(Time: 15 mins, Servings: 8)

Dry Ingredients

1 pack brioche hotdog buns
1 cup feta cheese crumbles
3 mangos, diced
1 red bell pepper, diced
½ red onion, diced
¼ cup cilantro, chopped
1 jalapeño, diced
½ tsp sea salt
½ tsp ground garlic

Wet Ingredients

1 pack all-beef hotdogs
2 limes, ¼ cup lime juice
8 tbsp hot honey
2 tbsp salted butter, melted

Directives

1. In a large bowl, add mango, bell pepper, onion, cilantro, and jalapeño. Pour lime juice over mixture and stir. Salt to taste. Set aside.
2. Set oven to broil and preheat grill or stovetop skillet to medium-high heat.
3. In a small bowl, mix melted butter and ground garlic.
4. Grill hotdogs until skin has darkened and is slightly wrinkled, 5-7 minutes.
5. While hotdogs are grilling, place buns on a cookie sheet, brush with garlic butter, and broil for 3 minutes.
6. Spoon 1 tbsp hot honey onto seam of broiled bun, place grilled hotdog atop honey, top with mango salsa and feta cheese crumbles. Repeat with each hotdog and enjoy.

Mash(ed) Mutton

(Active Time: 3 hours, Total Time: 28 hours, Servings: 12)

Marinade

2 cups Greek yogurt
½ cup brown sugar
¼ cup cilantro, chopped
3 tbsp ginger paste
2 tbsp garlic paste
1 tbsp ground cinnamon
1 tbsp sea salt
2 tsp black pepper
1 lemon, 4 tbsp lemon juice

Roast

6 lbs bone-in mutton leg
2 lbs red potatoes, halved
1 lb carrots, peeled & chopped
2 yellow onions, quartered
2 cloves garlic, minced
1 lemon, 2 tbsp lemon juice

Directives

1. In a large bowl, combine marinade ingredients and mix until smooth.
2. Place mutton leg into roasting pan and score thickest sections deeply.
3. Completely coat the mutton in marinade. Then cover the roasting pan with lid or foil and refrigerate for 24 hours.
4. Remove mutton from fridge 1 hour prior to cooking.
5. Preheat oven to 350°F.
6. Add potatoes, carrots, onions, and garlic to roasting pan, cover with foil, and bake for 2.5 hours, basting once halfway through.
7. Remove roast from oven, pour lemon juice over the top, and enjoy.

Chaperone Pie

(Active Time: 1.5 hours, Total Time: 26 hours, Servings: 6)

<u>Crust</u>

2 ½ cups all-purpose flour
2 sticks unsalted butter, cold
8 tbsp water, ice-cold
1 tbsp granulated sugar
½ tsp sea salt

<u>Filling</u>

5 cups fresh cherries, pitted
¾ cup granulated sugar
¼ cup tapioca starch
1 lemon, 2 tbsp lemon juice
1 tbsp unsalted butter, sliced
1 tbsp whole milk
1 tbsp pure vanilla extract
1 tsp almond extract
1 large egg

Directives a la Crust

1. Add flour, sugar, and salt into food processor and pulse to combine. Add cold butter slices and pulse for 30 seconds.
2. Scrape mixture into a large bowl and mix in water, 1 tbsp at a time, until dough has formed. Avoid overworking.
3. Split dough into two, shape into 1-inch-thick circles, cover in plastic wrap, and refrigerate for 24 hours.

Directives a la Pie

1. Preheat oven to 350°F.
2. Remove dough from fridge and roll out on a lightly floured surface. Each crust should be 12-inch in diameter to fit a 9-inch pie pan.
3. Place one rolled-out pie crust into pan and pierce throughout with a fork. Then place parchment paper atop pierced pie crust and pie weights atop parchment paper.
4. Bake pie crust for 15 minutes or until edges brown.
5. While pie crust is baking, combine all filling ingredients (except butter, milk, and egg) in a large bowl and stir until mixed.
6. Remove pie crust from oven and add cherry filling.
7. Raise oven temperature to 400°F.
8. Slice the second rolled-out pie crust into 1-inch strips. Lay half the strips, in the same direction, across cherry filling with equal spacing between. Weave remaining strips, perpendicular to the first, in an under, over, repeat pattern. Trim excess, press ends into bottom crust, and flute.
9. In a small bowl, beat the egg yolk and milk. Brush the egg wash over the pie crust and sprinkle with sugar. Place butter slices atop filling between the lattice crust.
10. Bake pie on center rack for 50 minutes or until filling begins to bubble. Once bubbling, cook 5 more minutes.
11. Remove pie from oven, cool, and enjoy.

Minty Male-Meltdown

(Time: 2.5 hours, Servings: 8)

Dry Ingredients

1 cup granulated sugar
1 cup semi-sweet chocolate chips
1 tsp sea salt

Wet Ingredients

2 cups whole milk
2 cups heavy cream
1 tbsp pure vanilla extract
1 tsp pure peppermint extract
3 drops green food coloring

Directives

1. In a large bowl, combine all ingredients (except chocolate chips) and stir until smooth.
2. Pour mixture into pre-frozen KitchenAid ice cream bowl and begin churning on lowest speed.
3. 10 minutes into churn, add chocolate chips. Continue churning for 20 more minutes or until ice cream has thickened.
4. Scrape ice cream into an air-tight container, freeze for 2 hours, and enjoy.

meet the author

Luz Evan Kanin is a lifelong reader and lover of fictional worlds. After growing up in Texas, she packed her things and moved across the country to live along the waves of the Atlantic.

These days she can usually be found pounding blueberry cake donuts, munching on chips and queso, slurping ramen, *or* taking cold brew to the dome.

On the rare occasion she's not stuffing her face, hot girl walking under the sun, or being an embarrassment on social media, Luz busies herself crafting the worlds only reachable through ink and dreams.

all titles by Luz

<u>Mindless Among Us</u>

all the shops in charlotte are closed
all the airports in atlanta are closed
all the motels in memphis are closed

<u>Heir of Ever</u>

Kingdom of Time
Realm of Ruin (Dec 2026)
Chasm of Chaos (Dec 2027)

Kitchen of Time

Let's Get Social

Shop Now